TOMMY DONBAVAND

My Teacher

Ate My Brain

From the bestselling
author of
SCREAM STREET

EDGE

TOMMY DONBAVAND

My Teacher Ate My Brain

EDGE
W FRANKLIN WATTS

LONDON·SYDNEY

Part of the **RIVETS** series

This edition published in 2012
by Franklin Watts

Text © Tommy Donbavand 2012
Cover design by Peter Scoulding

Franklin Watts
338 Euston Road
London NW1 3BH

Franklin Watts Australia
Level 17/207 Kent Street
Sydney, NSW 2000

A CIP catalogue record for this book
is available from the British Library.

Nicholas Kinney/Shutterstock: front cover c.
Anastasiya Zalevska/Shutterstock: front cover tl,bl, tr, br.

ISBN: 978 1 4451 1467 5

1 3 5 7 9 10 8 6 4 2

Printed in Great Britain

Franklin Watts is a division of Hachette Children's Books,
an Hachette UK company.
www.hachette.co.uk

For Guy N. Smith,
author of Night of the Crabs,
the horror story that started it all...

Contents

Chapter One

I ran as fast as I could, my bare feet sinking in the soft sand, making it difficult to pick up speed. Behind me, I could hear the wet-throated scream of Miss Edwards, my maths teacher

— or, at least, what was left of
her. A glance over my shoulder
confirmed what I feared — she
was gaining on me. Her jaw,
broken in the fight, hung loose
and swung from side to side with
each of her uncertain strides. If
it wasn't for the blood cascading
down the exposed white bone of
her chin, it would have looked as
though she was yawning.

Miss Edwards had always
been good looking — the type of
teacher fancied by older students
and male staff alike. Her long,

blonde hair always had that "just been washed" look to it, and she smelled like a spring day — all honey and strawberries. Boys actually fought to sit at the front in her maths classes — and my best mate, Callum, never let me forget the day I absent-mindedly doodled her name in my exercise book. He said I had a crush on her — but that was just stupid.

Miss Edwards didn't smell of strawberries any more.
She smelled of rotten meat.
Of terror. Of death.

Her hair was matted with blood and lumps of grey that I knew had to be one of my classmate's brains. I had to get away.

Suddenly, my foot caught in a hole and a lightning bolt of pain shot up from my ankle as it twisted violently to one side. I fell, face first, into the sand, and for a second I almost gave up. I almost lay there and let Miss Edwards finish me off. But then I realised I was clutching something in my hand and I lifted my head to see what it

was. I was still holding the spatula
Mr Blake had handed me ready to
cook sausages on the barbecue.
I watched in fascination as the
moonlight glinted on its shining,
metal surface.

GLARK!

I flipped myself over onto my
back at the sound — just in time
to see Miss Edwards's twisted
face plunge down, teeth aimed
squarely for my throat. I lashed
out with the spatula as hard as I
could, and caught her in the side
of the face. The blow was enough

to knock her to one side — but
also enough to snap the head
from the spatula. Now all I had
was a jagged metal stick in my
hand. And that was probably what
saved me.

Miss Edwards loomed back
over me, a mixture of her blood
and saliva spattering down on
my cheeks like warm, sticky
rain. Her eyes — milky and
unfocussed — gazed down at me
hungrily. And then I knew what
I had to do. Placing the heel of
my hand against the bottom of

the spatula's handle, I pushed
the sharp end as hard as I could
into one of her eyes. Her eyeball
popped — I actually heard it —
and then all resistance was gone.

The metal spear sank deep into
Miss Edwards's brain and, with
a final groan, her lifeless body
slumped down on top of me. I
turned my head to one side —
partly to catch my breath and
partly so that I didn't have to look
at what i'd just done.

Then...

FLASH!

My vision flooded with white light and it was a few seconds before I could see clearly again. Slowly, everything came back into focus and I saw Callum kneeling in the sand beside me — his phone in his hand. He'd taken a photo of me and the corpse of Miss Edwards!

"Whoooo-ooo!" he said, grinning like an idiot. "Josh finally gets the chance to cuddle his favourite teacher!"

Chapter Two

By the time I pushed Miss
Edwards's corpse off me, Callum
was gone — racing along the
beach, shouting that he was going
to "find someone else who was
dressed up as a zombie". Could

he really think this was all make-believe? He'd seen the way I'd had to finish off Miss Edwards, and he still didn't understand this nightmare was real! Mind you — I was having a hard time believing it myself.

Things like this weren't supposed to happen in real life — and especially not on school camping trips. This morning, I was just one of five kids from Liverpool who stayed after school a couple of times a week to help out with the homework club — but now I was fighting the undead on a tiny island off the coast of Wales. This weekend away was the teachers' way of saying thanks for all our hard work — and Mr Blake had even arranged for us to stay here on Shell Island before it officially opened to visitors. He'd showed us on the map that it wasn't really an island, but when the tide came in and flooded the road, the camp site was cut off from the mainland until —

"ARGH!"

The sound jerked me back to my senses, and I quickly remembered that I was out in the open. Miss Edwards might be finally dead, but Mr Blake was still out here somewhere, hungrily searching for human flesh. I stood, taking care not to put too much weight on my twisted ankle. It hurt, but not enough to keep me from searching for somewhere to hide.

I hurried up the beach and over the sand dunes to the main camping ground. I knew our

flimsy tents wouldn't provide
any protection, but I was sure I'd
spotted a small concrete shed.
The moon was ducking in and out
from behind a gathering bank of
clouds and it was difficult to see
but — yes! There it was!

I half-ran, half-stumbled
across the camp site to the shed.
I fell against the rough stone
wall and took a moment to
catch my breath. Then I began
to circle the building, looking for
the door. In the distance, I could
just make out the orange glow

of the fire we'd started on the beach to cook dinner. Mr Blake had dug a pit and filled it with wood and clumps of dried grass, and he was just setting it alight when that thing — whatever it was — had risen up out of the sand and bitten him.

My fingers moved from concrete to wood. I'd found the door! If I was right, this would be the place where the site's groundskeeper kept all his tools — tools which could be used as weapons against anything or anyone that wanted to eat me. Thankfully, the door was unlocked and I quietly slipped inside the shed… where a hand grabbed me by the throat and shoved me hard against the wall.

"Listen to me, you brain-sucking scum! There's no way I'm going to let you eat the contents of my head or anyone else's, get it?!"

I caught a glint of metal in the thin shaft of moonlight that crept in through the single, filthy window. I knew the owner of that voice — and she was holding a pair of gardening shears!

"Lydia!" I cried. "It's me — Josh!"

There was a CLICK, and the powerful beam of a torch was aimed at my face.

"I know who it is," snarled Lydia. "I just don't know if you're safe to be around."

"I... I am!" I stammered as her grip tightened around my throat. "I haven't been bitten!"

Lydia's eyes glinted angrily in

the torchlight as she brought the shears closer to my face.

"Prove it!"

Chapter Three

I blinked in the torchlight.
"You want me to prove I'm
not a zombie?"

"Exactly!"

"Well, I know we're both in
serious danger, and I haven't tried

to rip your face off yet — how's that for proof?"

With a sigh, Lydia relaxed her grip and slumped to the floor. "Sorry," she said. "I just had to be sure."

"It's OK," I said, rubbing at my throat. Then I heard a sob. "Who's that?"

Lydia swung the torch round to reveal a second girl hunched up in the far corner. Her dress was torn and her face was streaked with tears.

"Amy!" I said, hurrying over. "Are you OK?"

"She won't answer," said Lydia. "She hasn't said a word since I dragged her away from the beach. I think she's in shock."

"I'm not surprised," I said, taking off my jacket and wrapping it around Amy's shoulders. It wasn't much, but it might help her to stop shivering. "What was that thing that bit Mr Blake?"

"Who knows?" said Lydia. "It looked like some sort of half-human, half-crab thing, but I didn't hang around to look."

"Me neither."

"Have you seen the others?" Lydia asked. "Did Miss Edwards get away?"

I shook my head. "Mr Blake attacked her and she became... one of them."

"He got Daniel, too," said Lydia. "So that means there are three of those things out there."

"Two, actually," I said, wiping the sticky remains of an eyeball from my cheek. "Miss Edwards isn't a problem any more."

"What about Callum?"

I almost laughed. "He's having a great time!"

"What?!"

"He thinks it's all a set up by Mr Blake and Miss Edwards to scare us," I said. "Like some sort of ultimate campfire horror story."

"Moron!"

Callum might have been my best mate, but on this occasion, I couldn't disagree.

"So, what do we do now?" I asked. "We can't stay in here forever."

Lydia thought for a moment. "Have you got your phone?"

I rummaged through my pockets, but they were empty. "I must have dropped it when I was fighting with Miss Edwards. How about you?"

"I have, but the battery's dead. And I think Amy left hers in the tent before we went out."

"Callum's got his phone

with him," I said, suddenly remembering the flash as he took the picture of me. "But he's probably skipping along the beach, looking for fairies."

"We'll have to try and get back to the tents, then," said Lydia. "If we can find Amy's phone, we can call — "

SMASH!

We ducked as the shed window exploded inwards, showering us with broken glass. I could see someone moving around outside.

"It's Mr Blake!" I hissed. The teacher's arm forced its way through the lethal shards and a bloodied hand groped in the air to try and find us.

"Perfect!" said Lydia. "That's better than getting to a phone!"

I stared at her. "How is a zombie finding us better than calling for help?!"

"He might have the minibus keys in his pocket!"

It took me a second to take in what Lydia was suggesting. "You want to ask him for his keys?"

"Not ask him, dimwit," Lydia snapped, ducking as Mr Blake's fingers brushed against her hair. "We'll have to take them from him by force."

"Then we'll need weapons."

I took the torch and swung it around the inside of the shed. Hanging on the walls were an assortment of tools. I chose a hefty gardening fork as Lydia gripped the handles of her trusty shears.

"Let's do it!"

Chapter Four

We burst out of the shed together,
screaming at the tops of our
voices. I don't know what the
screams added to the attack —
but it seemed to make us feel
better.

I ploughed into Mr Blake, shoulder first, sending him staggering backwards. I'd hoped to knock him to the ground, but he managed to stay on his feet and lunged at Lydia, hand outstretched. I heard her shears snap closed with a SHLINK, and four pink fingers dropped to the grass before us.

I stared at the detached digits in horror, almost expecting them to squirm around with lives of their own — but, of course, they didn't. They just lay there, spattered in blood. Mr Blake was gazing at his stump of a hand, wiggling his thumb from side to side as a mixture of blood and black goo streamed from where his fingers should have been. Then he attacked again.

This time, Mr Blake didn't get close enough for Lydia to use her shears. I stabbed him hard in the chest with my fork, the metal prongs sinking into his flesh and grating against the bones of his ribs. I pushed hard against the handle, knocking the teacher off his feet and onto his back.

I jumped onto Mr Blake's stomach
and put all my weight onto the
fork.

"Now!" I shouted to Lydia.
"Get the keys!"

Lydia dropped to her knees
and began to search through
Mr Blake's trouser pockets. The
creature beneath me finally
roared in anger and tried to force
himself up, but every movement
just caused the fork to sink lower
and lower into his chest.

FLASH!

I jumped as a burst of light hit us. It was Callum again.

"Wow!" he yelled in excitement. "Where did you get these made? They're so lifelike!"

He was picking up Mr Blake's severed fingers!

"Callum!" I barked. "Put those down and listen to me! This is not a joke — it's all real!"

The smile on Callum's face

faltered slightly as he glanced down at the fork in Mr Blake's chest, and then back up at me.

"Real?" he said, a slight tremor in his voice.

"Yes!" snapped Lydia. "Now, stop taking stupid pictures and help us!"

For a second, I really thought he believed us. Then another figure came lurching out of the darkness. It was Daniel, although I could only tell by the clothes he was wearing. Almost all of his face had been torn away, leaving behind a mass of red flesh.

"Brilliant make-up, Daniel!" cried Callum. He quickly took a picture of his advancing school friend, and then scampered off laughing to himself.

"Got them!" Lydia pulled a bunch of keys from one of Mr Blake's pockets. "Let's get to the minibus!"

I hesitated, even though Mr Blake was clawing at the leg of my jeans with his good hand and Daniel was shuffling in our direction — presumably attracted by the sound as he didn't appear to have any eyes left.

"What about Amy?"

Lydia shot a look back at the shed where her friend was still cowering.

"If we go back in there, we might never get out again. And if she stays quiet, they might not find her."

She was right. We had to leave Amy behind. I left the fork sticking out of Mr Blake's chest and we ran.

Chapter Five

Lydia grabbed the handle of the driver's door then paused, her breathing heavy.

"What's the matter?" I asked.

"I don't know how to drive," she admitted.

I'm nowhere near old enough to take my test yet, either, but I've driven the tractor on my uncle's farm a few times.

"I'll do it."

Lydia tossed me the keys and ran round to jump in the passenger seat. I started the engine, released the handbrake — and we were off.

We roared past the camp site's offices and the small shop and cafe — all locked up and dark — and we'd driven a couple of hundred metres along the causeway before the engine stalled. It was probably just as well; the tide was still in and covering the road. All I could see was black, churning water. One false move and we'd end up in the sea.

I turned the key, spinning the starter motor over. Nothing. I tried again. Just a groaning whirr. The engine wouldn't start.

"What are you doing?" demanded Lydia. I could hear the panic rising in her voice.

"I'm not doing anything."

"Start the engine!"

"It won't start!"

"We can't just sit here! They'll be coming after us! We have to —"

FLASH!

Christ! It was Callum again! He'd jumped up on the bonnet of the minibus and was grinning at us through the windscreen. He looked like a monkey climbing over a car at a safari park.

Lydia swung her door open.

"Get in here, you cretin!" she
screamed.

Callum jumped down into the
knee-high water and clambered in
past her.

"This is awesome!" he shrieked
happily. "Come on, whose idea
was it? I bet it was Daniel's,
wasn't it? He's always been into
drama!"

Then Lydia screamed. Before
she could close the door, a hand
plunged inside the minibus
and grabbed her by the arm. I
clutched at the neck of her T-shirt

and pulled back as hard as I could but whoever had hold of her arm was clearly stronger than me and I felt the material begin to rip.

"HELP ME!" Lydia sobbed as she was dragged slowly but steadily out into the darkness. I tried. I really did. But her T-shirt simply gave way. I couldn't save her...

Lydia disappeared into the gloom outside the minibus with a final choking scream. All I could do was reach across and slam the door closed behind her.

Outside, in the headlights, I

could see Mr Blake, Daniel and
Amy — oh no — they'd got Amy,
too — as they pushed Lydia down
out of sight and fell on top of her,
mouths wide and dripping with
drool.

FLASH!

And Callum was taking bloody
photos of the whole thing!

I spun round in my seat to face
him and snatched the phone out
of his hands.

"Stop it!" I yelled, tears
burning my eyes. "This isn't a
sodding game!"

SMASH!

The window behind my head
caved in and another hand snaked
inside. It grabbed my hair and
slammed my head back hard
against the metal of the door
again and again until I could feel
warm, sticky blood start to run
down my neck.

BANG!
BANG!
BANG!

The worst thing was, Callum
must have knocked the rear-view
mirror as he climbed into the

minibus, and I had a clear view of who was attacking me.

It was Miss Edwards.

The handle of the spatula still protruding from her burst eye, she snarled as she slammed my head back one final time.

BANG!
CRACK!

I heard my skull break and watched in silent shock as Miss Edwards worked her fingers into the break and pull the two halves of my head apart. I expected to

feel pain, to scream in agony —
but there was nothing. I guess
your body can only take so much
before it simply switches off.

On the back seat, Callum was
almost vibrating with excitement.

"I can't wait to post this stuff
online!"

He reached forwards and
snatched his phone back from the
front seat.

"I'm going to video this bit for
YouTube!"

I stared into the lens of his

camera phone as Miss Edwards
pushed her face into my exposed
brain and began to feast. Poor
Callum. Everyone thought he was
an idiot — except me. I didn't
think he was an idiot.

I thought he looked delicious.

About the author

When I was 12 years old, my dad took our family to a campsite off the west coast of Wales called Shell Island. We set up the tent, played football, had a barbecue, then got ready for bed.

I always read before going to sleep. A friend at school had lent me a book to take on holiday — *Night of the Crabs* by Guy N. Smith. I'd never read a horror novel before so I was quite excited as I switched on my torch and started Chapter 1.

I read the entire book that night. It had quite an effect on me.

You see, *Night of the Crabs* is about giant crabs that crawl out of the sea and eat people. Scary, huh?

Even scarier — it's about giant crabs that crawl out of the sea and eat people who are camping, just like me and my family.

I'll be more specific — *Night of the Crabs* is about giant crabs that crawl out of the sea and eat people who are camping ON SHELL ISLAND! The exact place where I was lying, helpless, in a sleeping bag, reading the book!

I've never been so scared in
my life, and I refused to go down
to the beach with my family
the following day in case I was
devoured by creepy crabs! But
the story stuck with me, and
it resulted in me going on to
read other horror books and,
eventually, to writing them.

That's why this book is set
on Shell Island, and why it's
dedicated to Guy N. Smith — the
author of *Night of the Crabs*. The
man who started it all...

Tommy Donbavand, August 2012

www.tommydonbavand.co.uk

Get in touch with Tommy
through his website.

DAVID GATWARD

BLOOD HOUSE

From the author of DOOM RIDER

EDGE

If you enjoyed reading My Teacher Ate My Brain,

you might also like BLOOD HOUSE,

by David Gatward.

Trev's sister is dead.
Trev's mum is dead, and his dad.

The authorities think he did it.
They won't believe him   that it was
the house that took them.

They won't believe him until it's too late and
there is only...
Blood red.
Torn flesh.
Red blood.

www.davidgatward.co.uk

Buy online at
www.franklinwatts.co.uk
978 1 4451 1467 5 paperback
978 1 4451 1470 5 eBook

Turn over to read an extract from

BLOOD HOUSE:

It was a motorcycle helmet that looked like it had barely survived a road accident.

Trev stared at his reflection in the mirrored visor. His eyes were black pools, empty, cold. Hunter's eyes.

"You were wearing it when they found you," said the doctor. "What about this?"

Trev had seen the photograph a thousand times: a normal hallway in a normal detached house in a normal part of the city. Except that this hallway looked like an abattoir. Something alive had been torn apart in that place, ripped limb from limb. Hadn't stood a chance.

"What happened to your family in this house, Trevor?"

Don't make me remember...

"Who did this?"

Not who, what...

"Was it you?"

Trev was off the bed in a beat. Like a tiger dragging its kill to the ground, he slammed the doctor onto the floor, winding him, knocking the helmet to skitter across the floor.

"They were my parents! My kid sister!" Trev spat, loud and desperate.

The gorillas yanked Trev away to restrain him.

"It was the bloody house!" he screamed, his skin burning against the rough hands holding him. "It took them! Why won't you believe me?"

Trev was crying now, with the pain of being held, the pain of the memory, the pain of knowing no one would ever believe him that the house had come alive. That it hadn't been a house at all, just something waiting for the right moment to spring the trap.
A beast hungry for blood.

The pinprick in the side of his neck came as no surprise.

The room melted to darkness.

To find out what happens to Trev, grab a copy of Blood House today!

Also available from **EDGE**.
CRIME TEAM adventures by the 2Steves,
where YOU crack the case!

978 0 7496 9283 4 pb
978 1 4451 0843 8 eBook

978 0 7496 9284 1 pb
978 1 4451 0844 5 eBook

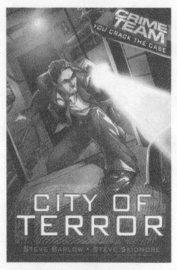

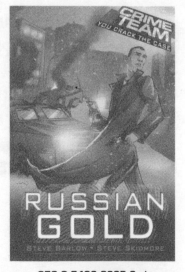

978 0 7496 9286 5 pb
978 1 4451 0845 2 eBook

978 0 7496 9285 8 pb
978 1 4451 0846 9 eBook